I AM NOT A
GHOST

◆

THE CANADIAN PACIFIC RAILWAY

While *I Am Not A Ghost: The Canadian Pacific Railway* is a work of fiction, it is based on a real event in history: the building of the Canadian Pacific Railway (CPR). Thousands of Chinese workers came to Canada to work on the railway, but the characters in this story are, for the most part, fictional, with one exception: Amelia Douglas, a Métis woman. Her mother was Cree and her father was Irish Canadian. She was married to James Douglas, who was the Governor of British Columbia from 1858 to 1864. His background was Scottish and Creole. They had thirteen children, only six of whom survived.

Amelia Douglas was a determined, helpful person whose caring and compassion for others was well known. After her husband died in 1877, she remained involved with her family and community until her death in 1890.

Photo credits—endpaper: Picksell/Shutterstock, 34: border—Riverway/Shutterstock, 36: top and bottom—Courtesy of Libraries and Cultural Resources Digital Collections, University of Calgary. 37: top—Image D-07548, bottom—Image C-06727—Courtesy of the Royal BC Museum, all other decorative borders: Picksell/Shutterstock.

www.plumleafpress.com

23 24 25 26 27   5 4 3 2 1

ISBN 978-1-7782428-1-6

Printed in China

I AM NOT A GHOST

THE CANADIAN PACIFIC RAILWAY

DAVID BOUCHARD

WITH ZHONG-YANG HUANG

ILLUSTRATED BY SEAN HUANG

For Gaga's Izabell
and for my amazing friend Zhong-Yang Huang,
who taught me so much about China
and through those teachings about my own country, Canada.

— David Bouchard

For my nephew, Kyzen

— Sean Huang

FOREWORD

In the early pages of this book, you will find perhaps its most important message. It is a place to pause and reflect on what you are about to read, especially if you are sharing this story with your own young family members or students.

Granddaughter, you and your children must know this story, and you must remember.

These powerful words are spoken by the main character, now a grandfather, as he is about to relate his experiences as a new immigrant to Canada, working on the final section of the Canadian Pacific Railway.

Although this book is described as a work of fiction, the majority of its content is wrapped around facts, as it chronicles the journey of the first Chinese Canadians.

My own maternal great-grandfather, Seto Fan Gin, arrived in British Columbia in 1862, five years before Canada's Confederation and only four years after British Columbia had been named as a crown colony, with James Douglas as its first governor. Seto Fan Gin brought his skills as a tailor with him and was soon in business making and selling sails and tents. The miners flocking to the Gold Rush in the Fraser Canyon and Cariboo regions would have been his primary customers at that time. By 1881, he may, in fact, have been making many of the canvas lean-tos mentioned in this book, intended to offer what shelter they could to the Chinese rail workers.

His son, my grandfather, Seto Ying Sek (Seto Moore), was a highly respected scholar, who was consulted as the Chinese Immigration Act of 1923 was being drafted. Although the Act was still passed into law, he can be credited with softening some of the limitations; his input meant some Chinese, such as merchants, were still allowed into Canada, although only by exception.

My paternal grandfather, Hok Yat Louie, arrived in British Columbia in 1898. Like the men in this book, he had little English and virtually no money after paying the required Chinese Head Tax. Just like the Chinese railway workers, he had a tremendous work ethic, drive, and passion. He was also possessed of incredible vision, one he never lost sight of, as he transitioned from farm labourer to Chinatown merchant to community leader. With few resources and no support, he created a family business that is still thriving almost 120 years later and in its fourth generation of family leadership.

In the book, Lady Amelia Douglas, the wife of Governor James Douglas, is depicted as a character full of compassion, just as she was in reality throughout her life. So it was with my grandfather, Hok Yat Louie, a man of great moral fibre and strong ethical beliefs as well as an inspiring role model. He stepped in to help hundreds of his fellow immigrants pay their head tax, never asking for repayment.

Some were able to repay their debt, while others were not; the tax by then was $500, the equivalent of three years' annual salary for most Chinese immigrants at the time.

My grandfather and his fellow immigrants would need that strong moral fibre as they navigated the entrenched systemic racism so evident in Canada at the time. They came here to fulfill a dream, just as immigrants have always done. They were thwarted at every turn, rejected, overlooked, and denied even the most basic of human rights. Yet they persevered. They withstood violence and destruction in 1907 when the Asiatic Exclusion League, a white supremacist group, attacked and tried to destroy their businesses.

Today, more than 100 years on from the Chinese Immigration Act of 1923 (also known as the Chinese Exclusion Act), you might assume that the racism levelled at Chinese Canadians then is non-existent today; you would be wrong. The Chinese were not granted full citizenship until 1947, which meant that my parents, my brother, and I, all born in Vancouver, were denied citizenship until that year. This may come as a surprise to many Canadians, who pride themselves on Canada's reputation for multiculturalism, but for many Asian Canadians, it is their life story.

The 2020 Covid pandemic did not *create* the issue of anti-Asian racism — it merely pulled back the covers on an issue that has always existed, albeit just under the surface. The power of telling our stories and those stories being heard is only one of the tools we have to combat racism; education is another, and books like this one serve that purpose admirably.

Winston Churchill once famously said: *The farther backward you look, the further forward you can see.*

My father, Tong Louie, taught me a valuable lesson when he said that we can choose to forgive, but we must never forget. In other words, we can choose not to be defined by what happens to us. We can and must move forward and create our own success in spite of the obstacles we encounter.

This is precisely why this book is so vital for all Canadians. I encourage you to share this book with your family, friends, schools, and community groups. Use it as the starting point for gathering your own knowledge of the history of Chinese Canadians. Make it a doorway to opening up new perspectives on how we must all remember and share our stories.

Canada is still writing its story as a nation, and this book is an important part of that story.

— Dr. Brandt C. Louie, Chairman and CEO of the H.Y. Louie Company Limited
    and ninth Chancellor of Simon Fraser University

"Johnny! You!

Johnny! GET UP!

You don't have all day to lie around!"

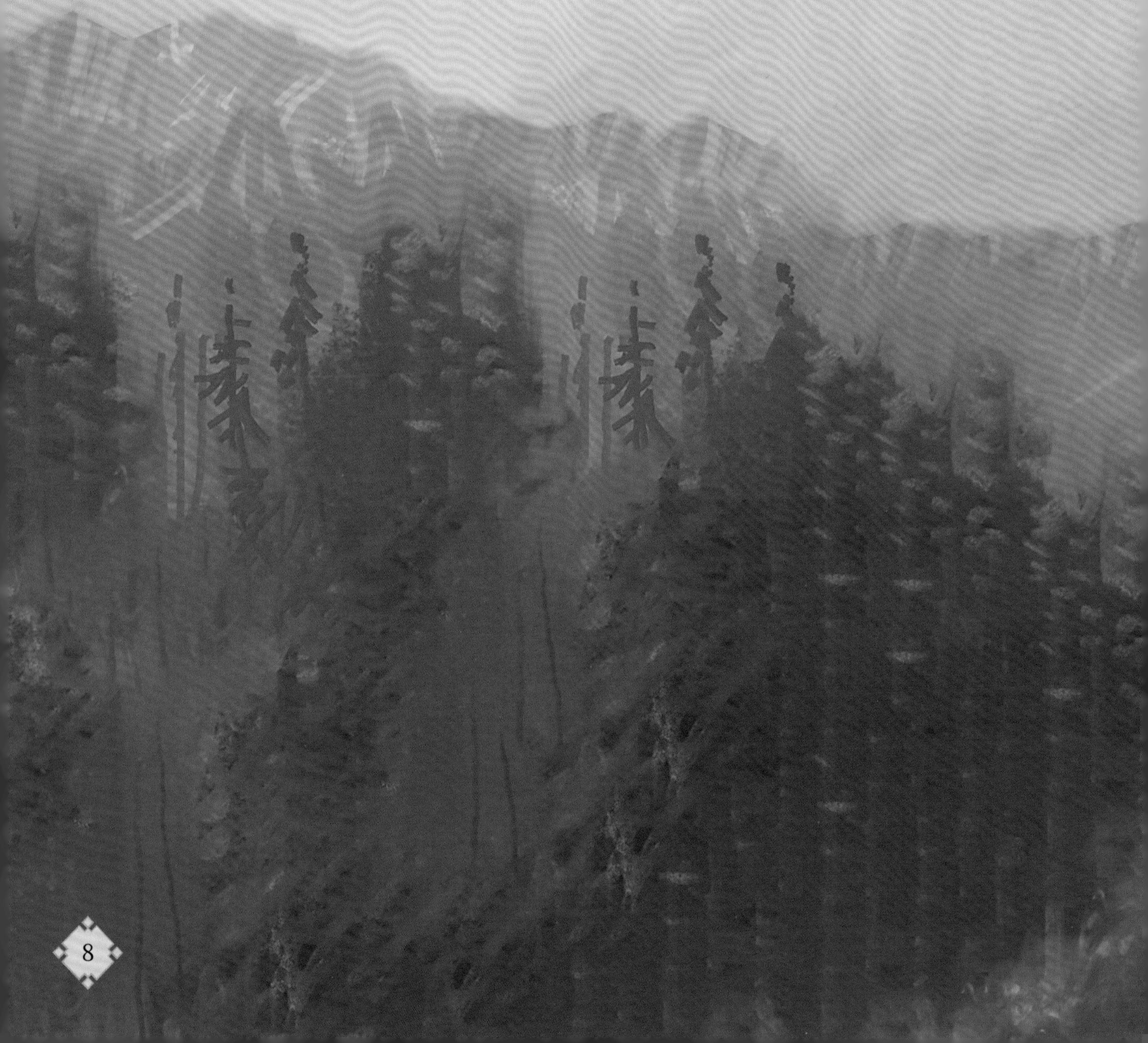

Even after all these years, the foreman's words are as clear in my mind today as they were then.

Granddaughter, you and your children must know this story, and you must remember.

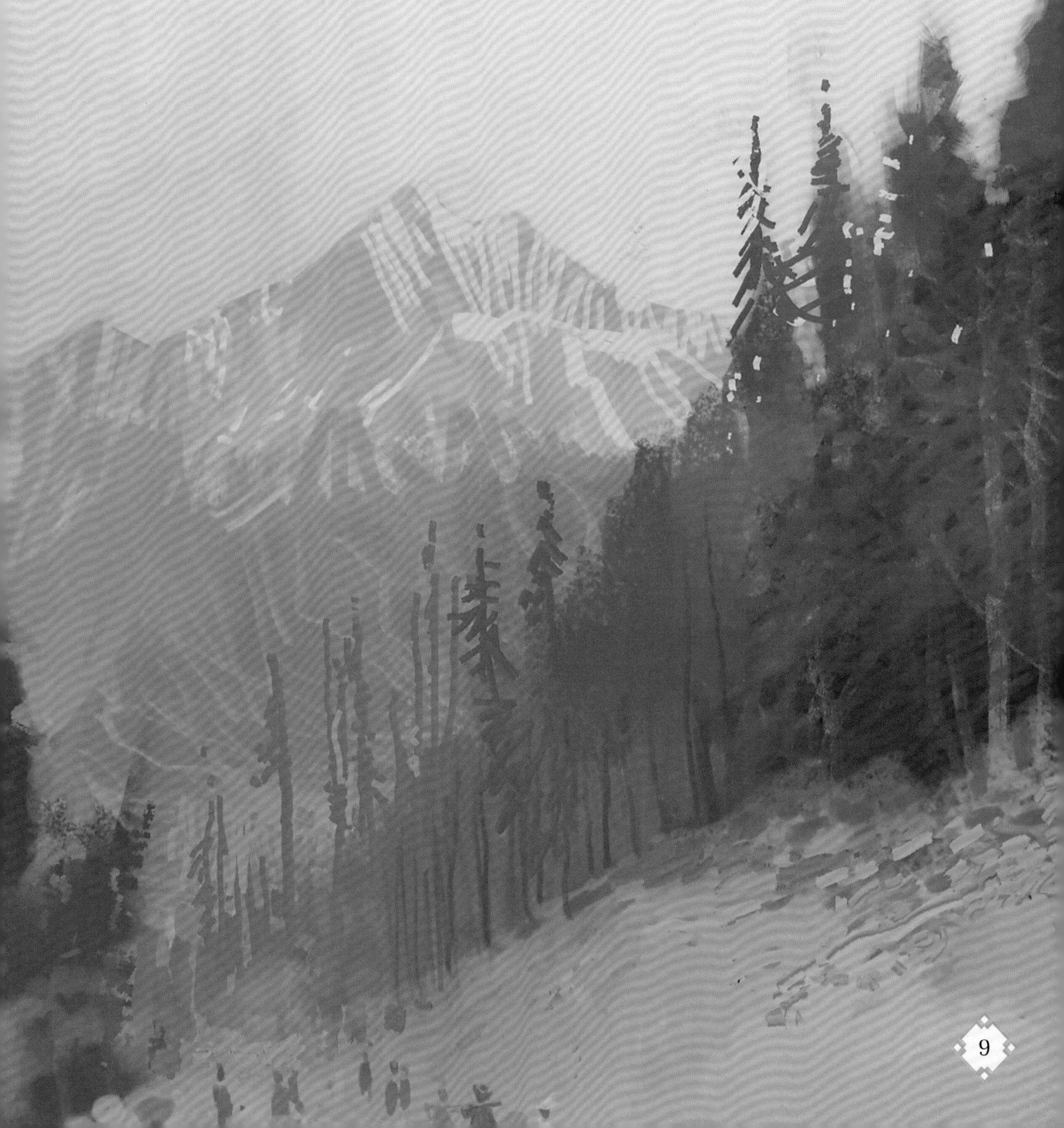

Life at home in China was extremely difficult. The Empress was cruel and harsh. Work had become next to impossible to find. So when I heard of the possibility of a new life here for me, my wife, and our baby son, I was excited.

I had heard that the trip across the ocean was long and treacherous. Yet, like so many of my countrymen, I dreamed of a bright future in this vast promised land.

I left my family and made the crossing. The voyage was indeed terrifying, and like all my countrymen on the ship, I was thankful when we sighted land, excited at the prospect of what lay ahead.

We soon learned the reality of life in the promised land.

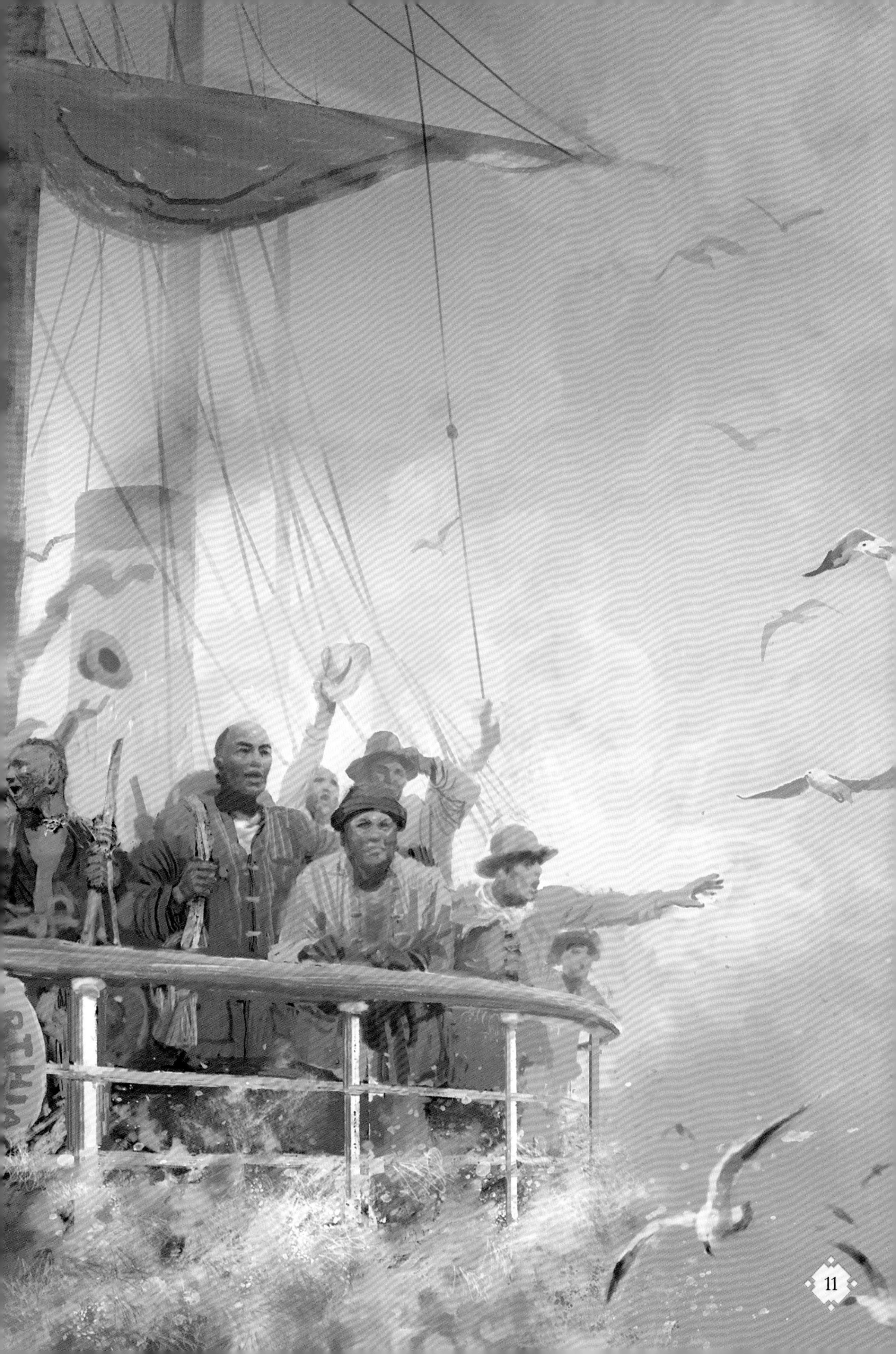

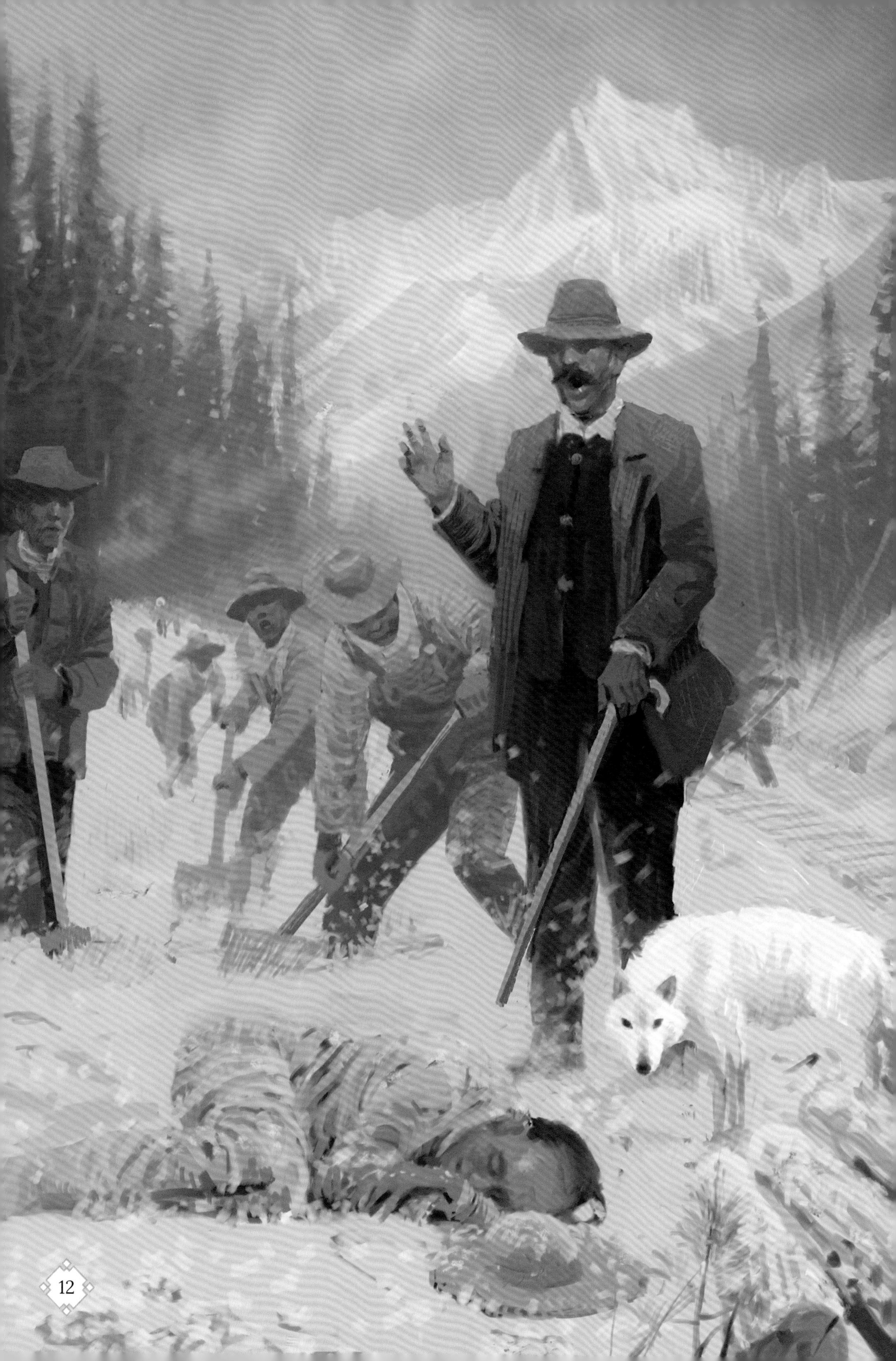

* * *

"Johnny" was the first word I heard when I arrived in Victoria. These white men thought all Chinese men looked the same. They called us all "Johnny" and never bothered learning our names.

And "Johnny" was what I heard as I lay on the frozen ground that day, next to a railway line on which I had toiled day and night for many months. I had collapsed from cold, hunger, and exhaustion. A bowl of rice once a day was not enough for any man, especially those like us who worked such long and hard hours building the railway. We could not afford any vegetables or fruits, and scurvy ran rampant among us. Many Chinese workers had already died on this stretch of railway line alone ... and for what? For one dollar a day? This was less than half the pay of a white worker and came to even less after paying for our own equipment and food. It was not fair and not right. Everyone knew this. This was certainly not the future I had come seeking. This was not the opportunity I had been promised! Yet, I saw a path that told of a bright and prosperous future. So I persisted — day by day — hour by hour.

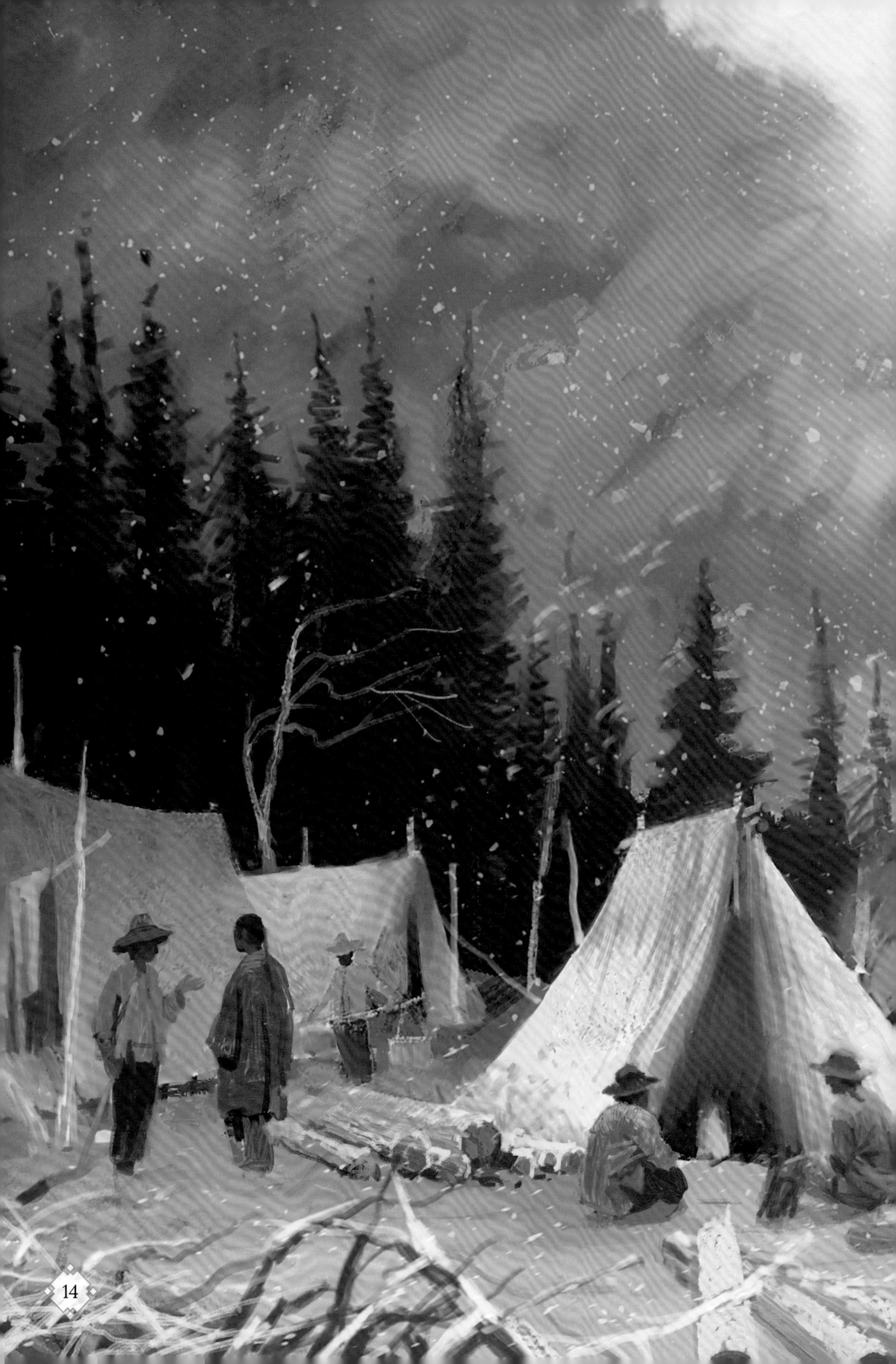

I was shocked by the harsh winters in Canada. I had never experienced such freezing temperatures and snowfalls in southern China.

Here, high in the Fraser Canyon, I was living under a canvas tarp. The lean-to I was assigned as my home provided little protection from the bitter cold, and none at all from falling rocks like the ones that crushed a worker two places over from mine the week before.

We had to work with explosives to blast a tunnel through the mountains. Many Chinese workers lost their lives working with faulty explosives. If there were any white workers working with dynamite, blasting rock, I never saw them. I had experience working with explosives back in China and was paid a little extra to work with dynamite.

After a few years, with the money I had saved, and with a lot of help from some benevolent Chinese immigrants, I was able to send for my wife and son. They arrived safely, and I found them a place to live in Victoria's Chinatown.

* * *

"Johnny, *GET UP!*" ... A kick from my foreman and then ...

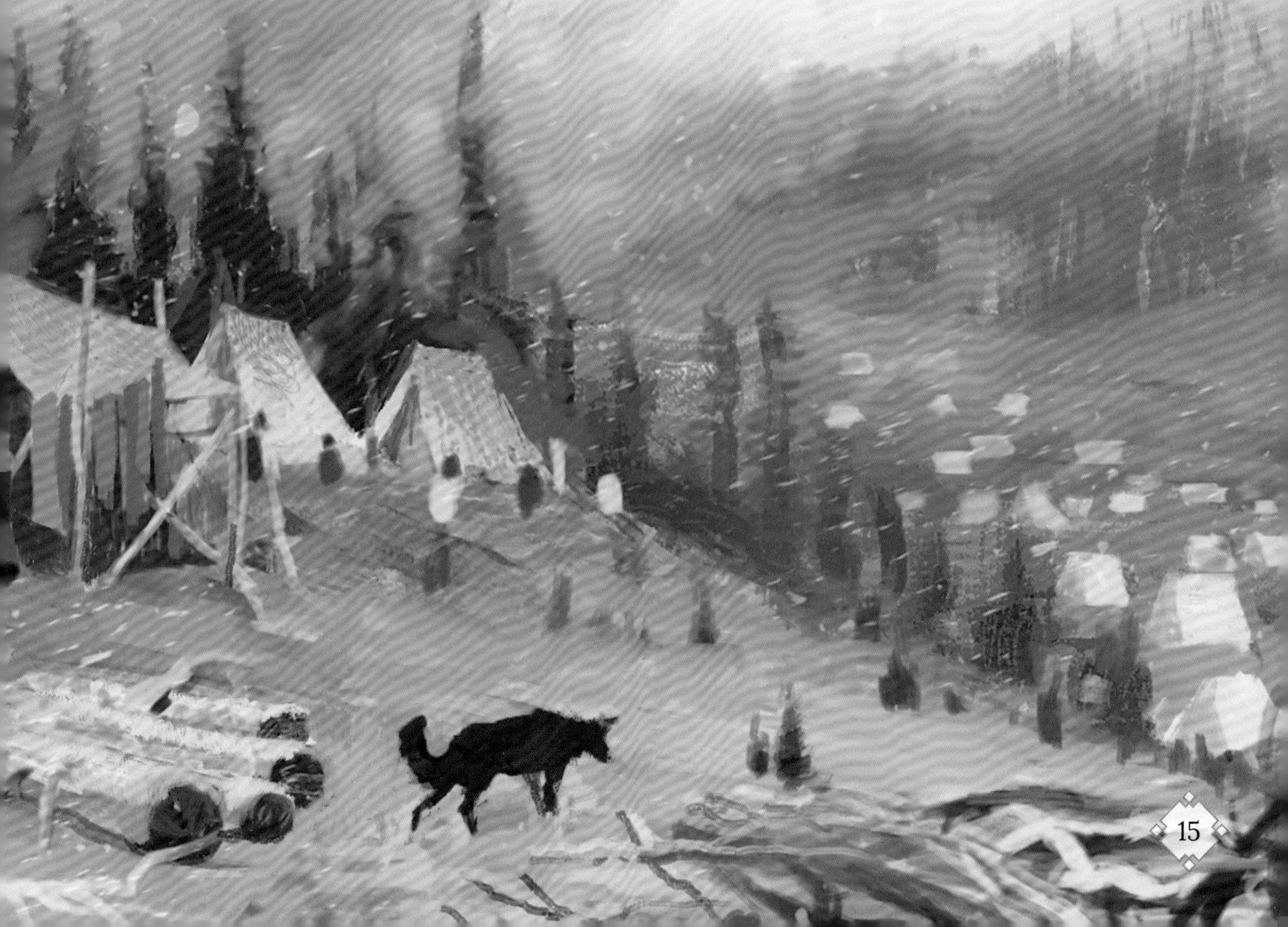

Some time must have passed. The next thing I heard was a woman's commanding voice.

"Does no one see this man?" she asked loudly.

No one answered.

"Excuse me! Does no one see this man?" The woman's voice was louder now. "He is obviously unwell."

I half turned, and through bleary eyes, I saw a tall, imposing woman standing nearby.

I could barely make out her words, but the tone of her voice allowed me to understand what was happening.

Those around her carried on talking and laughing, oblivious to her concern.

I heard a worker next to my foreman say, "Boss, that's Mrs. Douglas! Very important woman!"

The foreman finally replied. "Yes, I see him, Mrs. Douglas. But there is nothing for you to be concerned about. He's just a Johnny. He'll be fine. If he doesn't get up soon, I'll get someone to take him back to his shelter."

Then he added, "These Chinese workers are lucky to have this work. For them, it's a job and a chance to live in our beautiful country. They are very useful for us up here on the line. I figure that anyone who can build the Great Wall of China can surely build a railroad." Amused at his own humour, he laughed.

The woman did not.

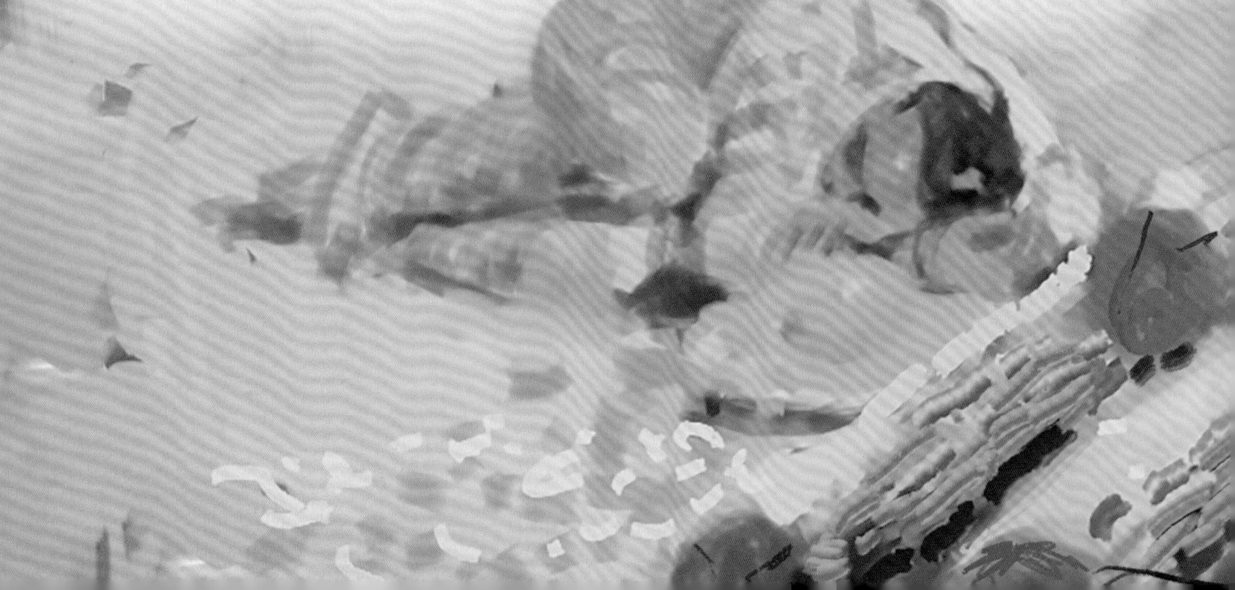

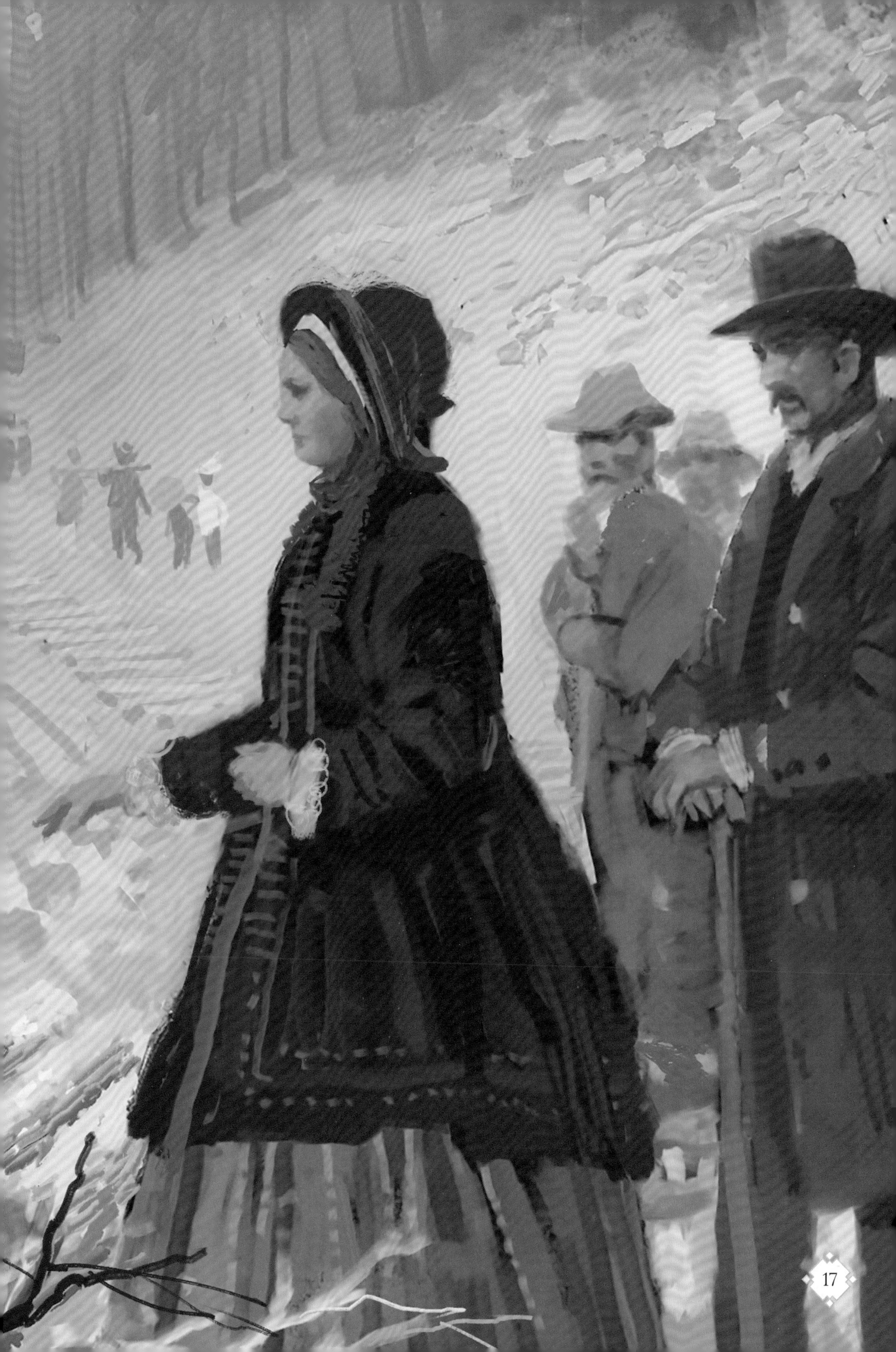

"Someone will come for him?" she asked. "And then what? What will become of him? What happens to these poor men when they become ill?"

The foreman answered, "Not something to concern yourself with, Ma'am. Believe you me, no one else does. But since you asked … It depends, I suppose. We lose a few, naturally. They die for all kinds of reasons, not the least of which are the diseases they bring with them from those horrible boats on which they sailed across the ocean. This one will be taken back to his shelter, and in all likelihood, he'll be back at work tomorrow. These Chinese workers have strong constitutions."

Exasperated, Mrs. Douglas persisted. "This man is very sick! Something has to be done for him. *Now!*"

The foreman shook his head as he replied, "Mrs. Douglas, if he's as sick as you think, he should have quit and left camp days ago. No one is keeping him here."

"*That*, Sir, is *not* good enough!" replied Mrs. Douglas. "I want this man placed on my cart *immediately*. I will take him home with me to be cared for as anyone should be."

Clearly irritated now, the foreman said, "I wouldn't if I were you, but I will not go against your wishes. Johnny knows the risks of working up here, and he's grateful to be here. But it's your decision, of course."

Then he yelled, "***Ben, fetch a few of the boys, and load him onto the back of Mrs. Douglas's cart.***"

As I was moved onto the flat of a horse-drawn cart, the foreman added, "I hope you know what you're getting yourself into, Ma'am. Chances are your Johnny here won't make the trip back to the city. In fact, he might already be dead."

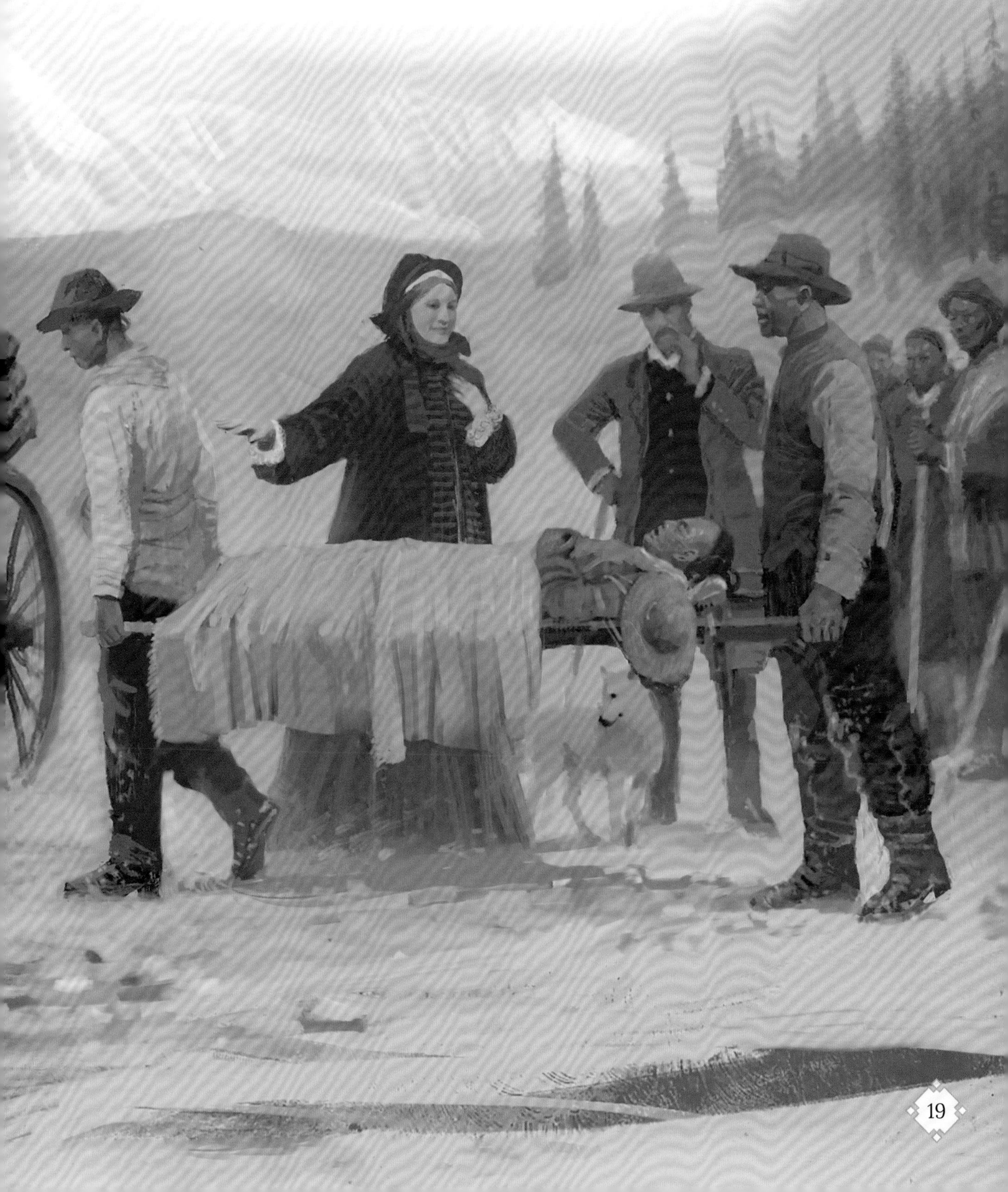

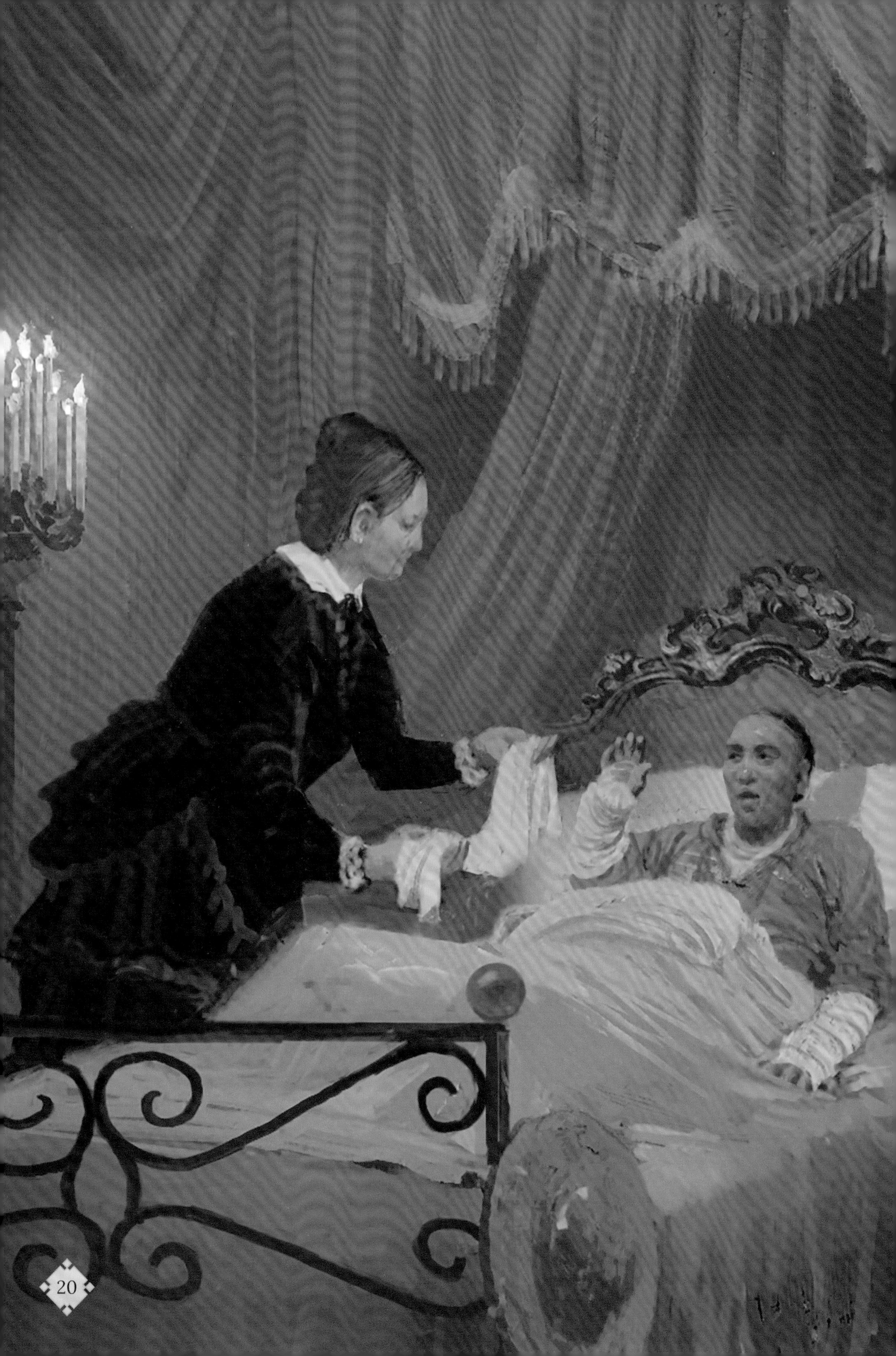

That was how I came to wake up in Victoria, in a strange bed, surrounded by people I did not know. My life was forever changed.

* * *

"Where am I?" I asked as I looked around a room unlike any I had ever seen before. It was huge and ornate, much like what I imagined the Empress's rooms to be.

Someone moved to the side of my bed, and I found myself looking at the woman who had rescued me.

"Where am I?" I asked. "Who are you?"

Her voice was calm and soothing. "I am Amelia Douglas. My husband was James Douglas, the Governor of British Columbia. I found you ill on the track line and brought you here, to our home."

She is the wife of the Governor? This is her home?

"Our family doctor has been treating you for a little over a week now. You seem to be getting stronger."

Struggling to get on my feet, I gasped. "A week? I cannot stay here any longer. I must go to my wife and son in Chinatown. They will not know where I am. I must go to them. I must go now!"

"That's not possible." She spoke with a voice of authority. "You will stay right where you are. I have staff who will go to Chinatown to get your wife and child. Your wife can work for me until you are completely better."

"Why are you doing this?" I asked. "I am poor. I have nothing to give you."

"All I want is to see you get better and back on your feet. Everyone should be treated fairly in this country."

Just as she said she would, Mrs. Douglas sent out people looking for your grandmother and your father. They found them alone, afraid, and hungry.

* * *

The following morning, I opened my eyes to find your grandmother and your father standing next to my bed.

I shook with excitement as your grandmother knelt beside my bed.

"They told us you were dead," she sobbed. "The men from the camp all said you had died." She stroked my face to be sure that it was really me — that I had not died. Your father called out, "Papa! Papa!"

When your grandmother finally stopped crying, I told her what had happened, as clearly as I could remember it.

Your grandmother spoke no English, but her eyes were filled with tears of gratitude as she sought out those of Mrs. Douglas. One of Mrs. Douglas's staff translated.

"I ... I do not know who you are or why you have done this, Ma'am, but you have saved three lives, not one. Our family will forever be grateful to you."

Mrs. Douglas had food and drink brought to us. She offered your father and your grandmother lodging. Your grandmother politely refused any more kindness as she had to get back to work at a laundry service in Chinatown. However, Mrs. Douglas would not hear of this. She insisted your grandmother and your father stay.

They stayed. I healed. We all healed.

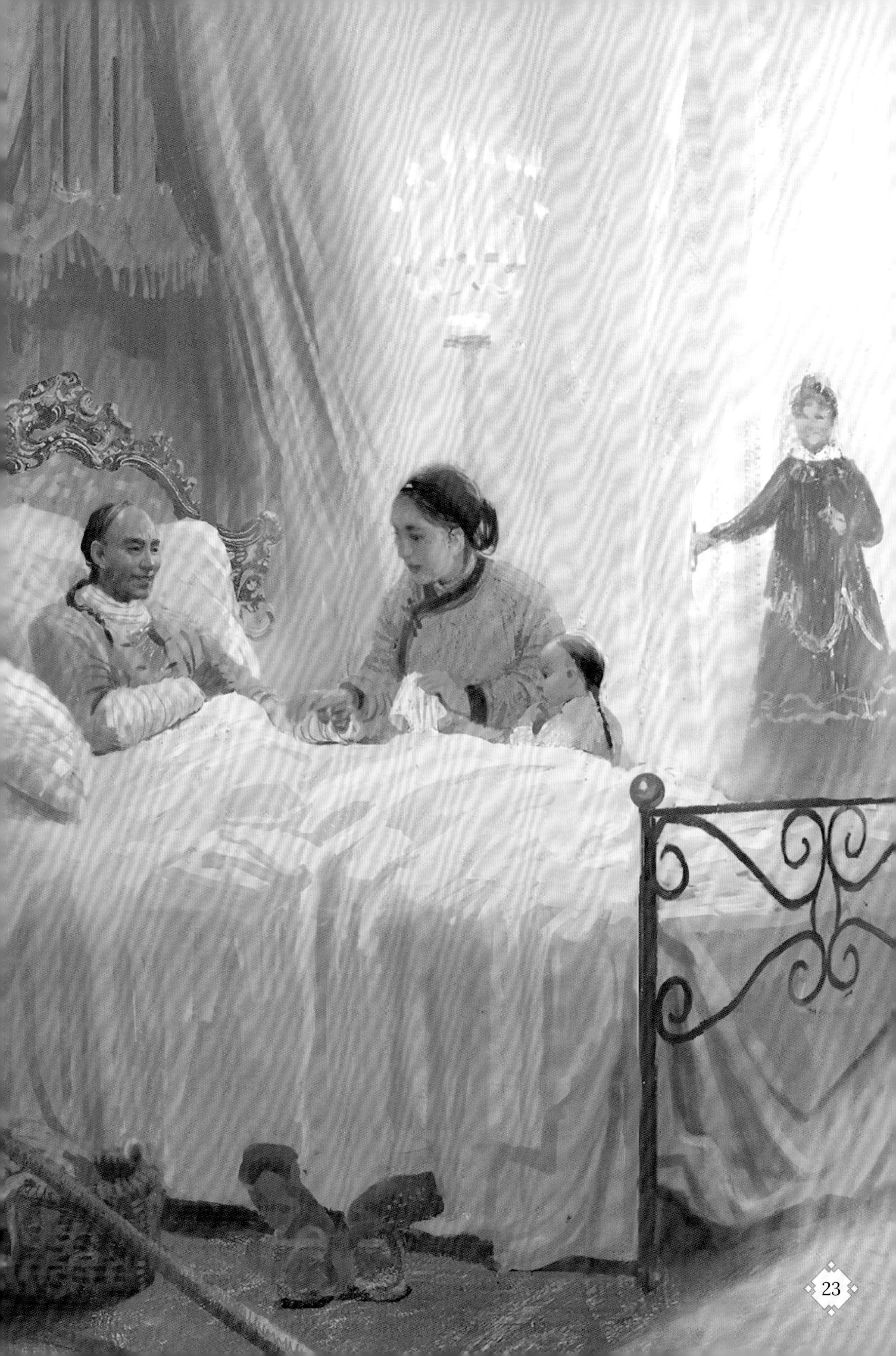

After three weeks, I was better. It was time for us to focus on our family's future, on our dream. I sought out Mrs. Douglas.

"Mrs. Douglas, we must leave. I am much stronger now, and I have to go back to work. We have friends in Chinatown who will look after my wife and son while I return to the railway line."

Mrs. Douglas looked concerned. "Are you sure you are strong enough to go back to work on the railway?"

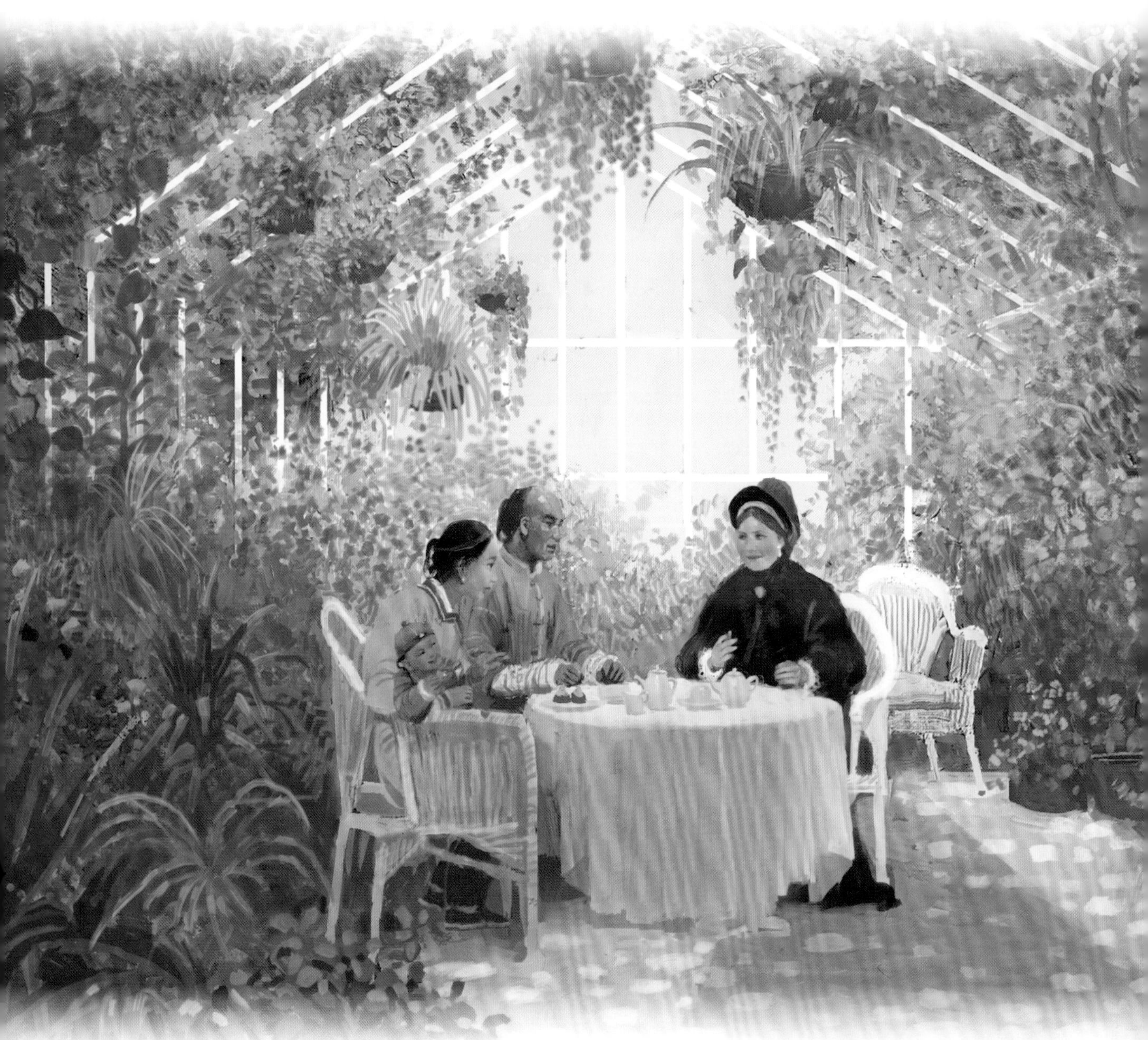

"Yes, Ma'am," I replied. "My work there is only temporary. I will soon have
enough money to start a business of my own. My father has a cousin in Canton
who is a trader. He would like a partner here in Canada to receive and market
his goods. I believe I can do well in the business."

Choking on my words, I continued. "I have no words big enough to express my
gratitude for all you have done for me and my family. Thank you is not enough.
You will forever live in our memory and in our hearts."

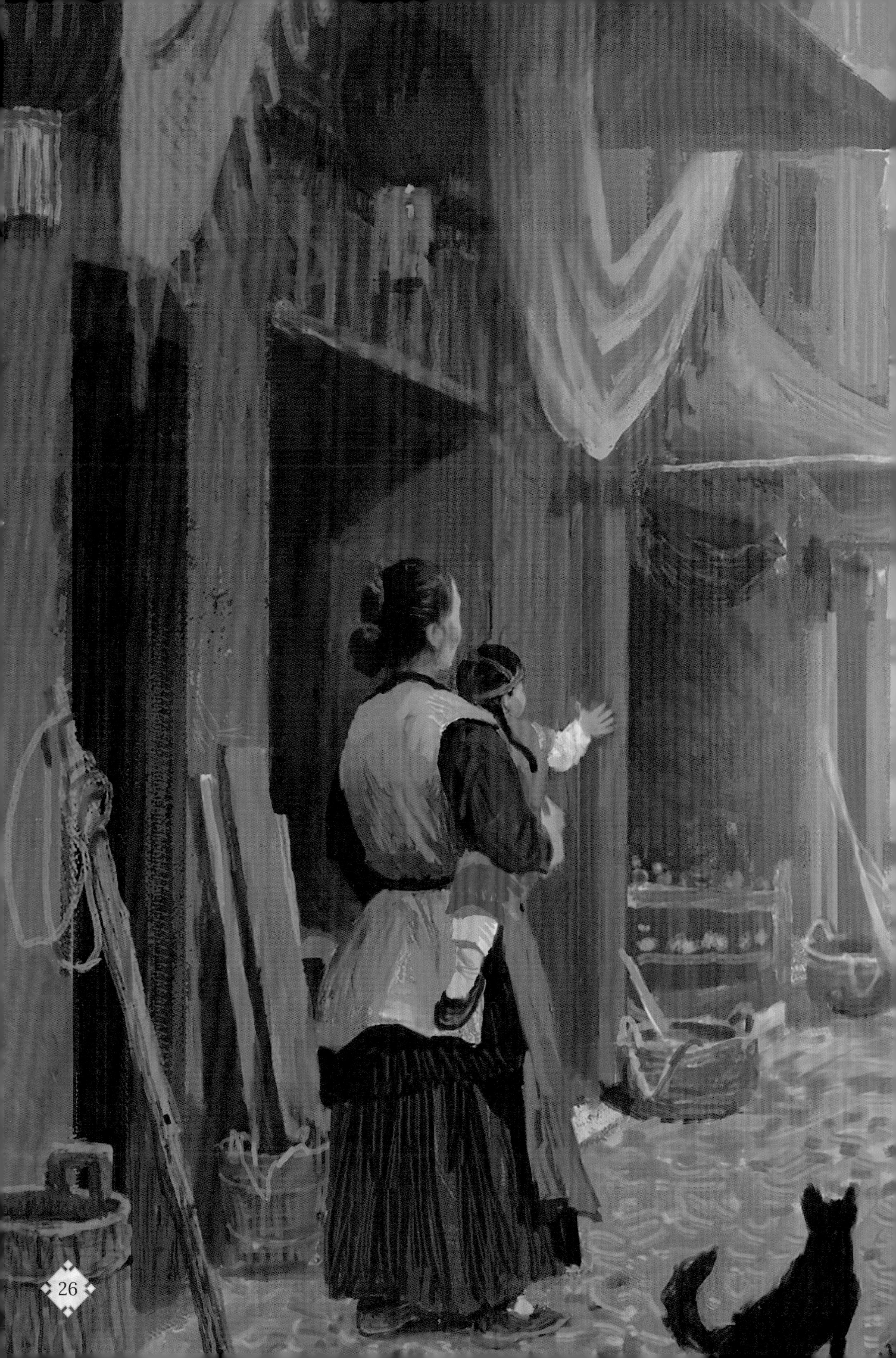

We returned to Chinatown. Nothing there had changed. We settled back into the Chinese community, and when I felt sure my family was safe and cared for, I returned to the railway line.

* * *

The foreman paid little attention to me as I walked back into the camp. Help was needed, and I appeared to be a healthy Johnny. He looked at me but did not recognize me as the man whom he had presumed dead only weeks before. He often said that all Johnnies looked alike.

"Hey Johnny, don't waste any time. Go on! Get moving!"

I headed up the track. As I walked, a strange thing occurred.

One by one, my countrymen raised their eyes and stared at me. Some dropped their tools. They shared the same fear as they all uttered, in hushed tones, one word — "*GHOST!*"

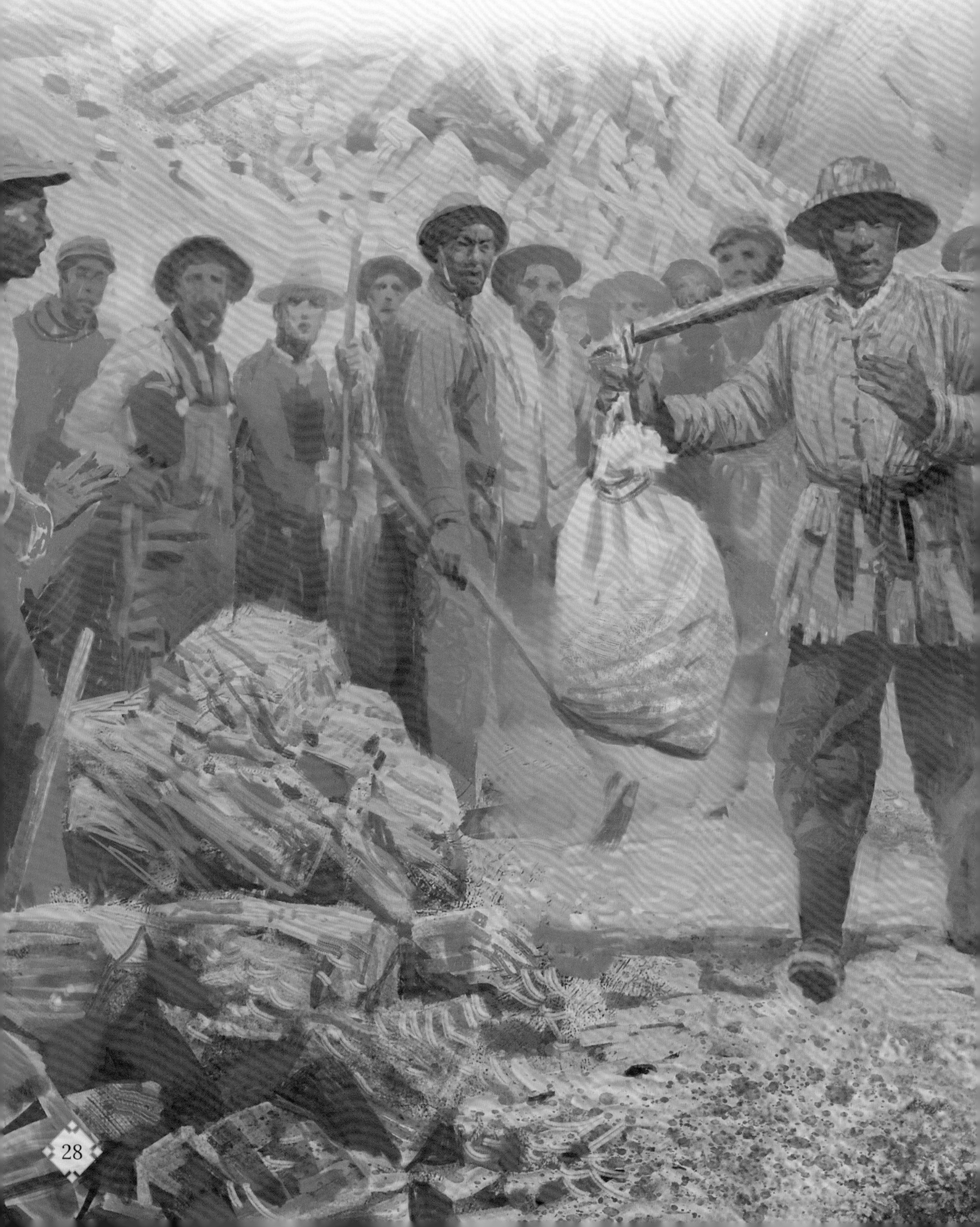

A pathway slowly opened up between them. I walked through it, and as I did, I spoke softly, saying,

"I am not a ghost! I live."

Over and over, I repeated,

"I am not a ghost! I live."

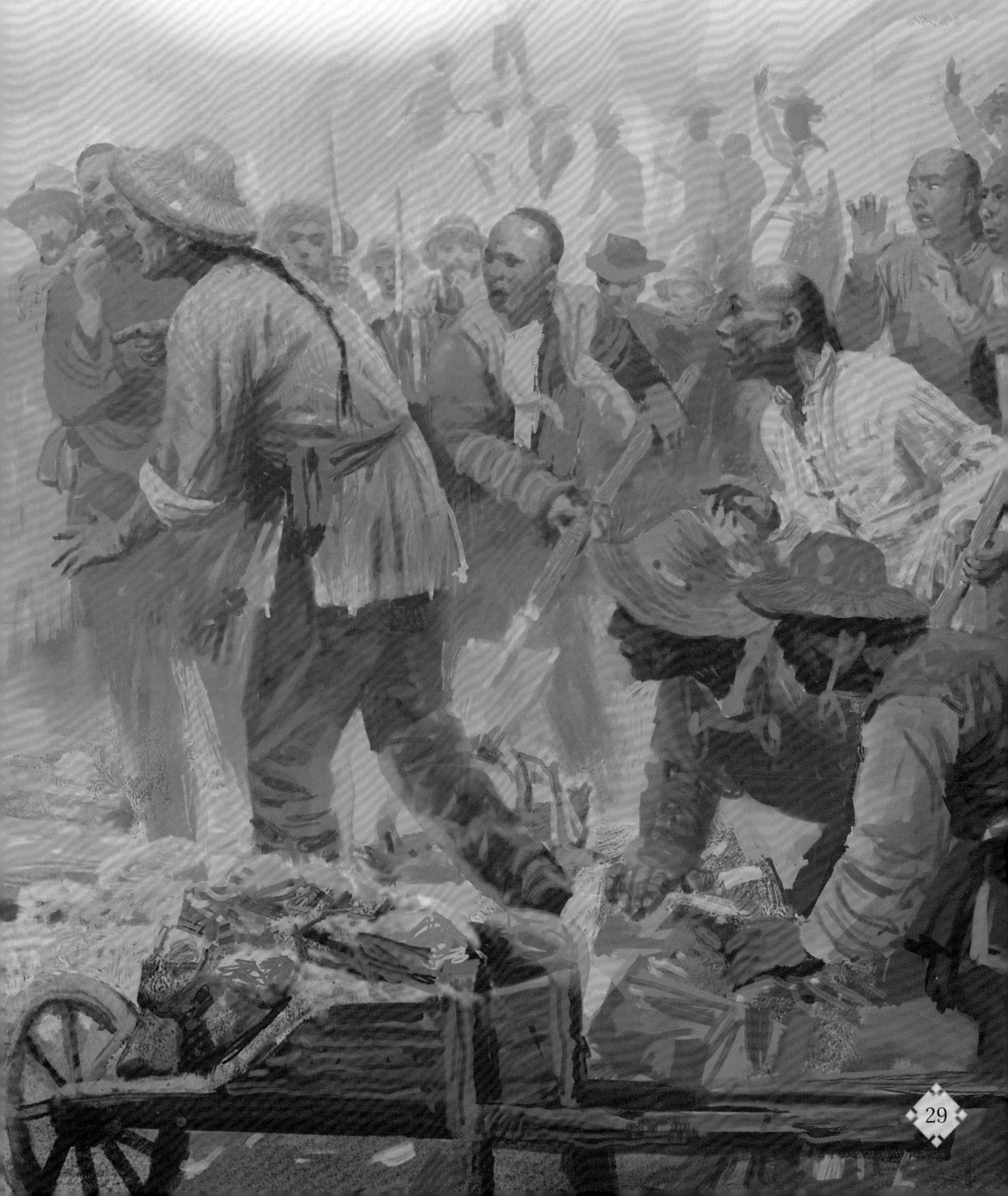

The other Chinese workers helped me settle back into the camp, pitching my tent and sharing their food on my first night back.

It took me several days to convince them that I had not died and that I was not a ghost. They wanted to know all about the woman who had dragged me from the clutches of death, and how she had helped me and my family. No one could believe that such a powerful person would care about the fate of a Chinese railway worker.

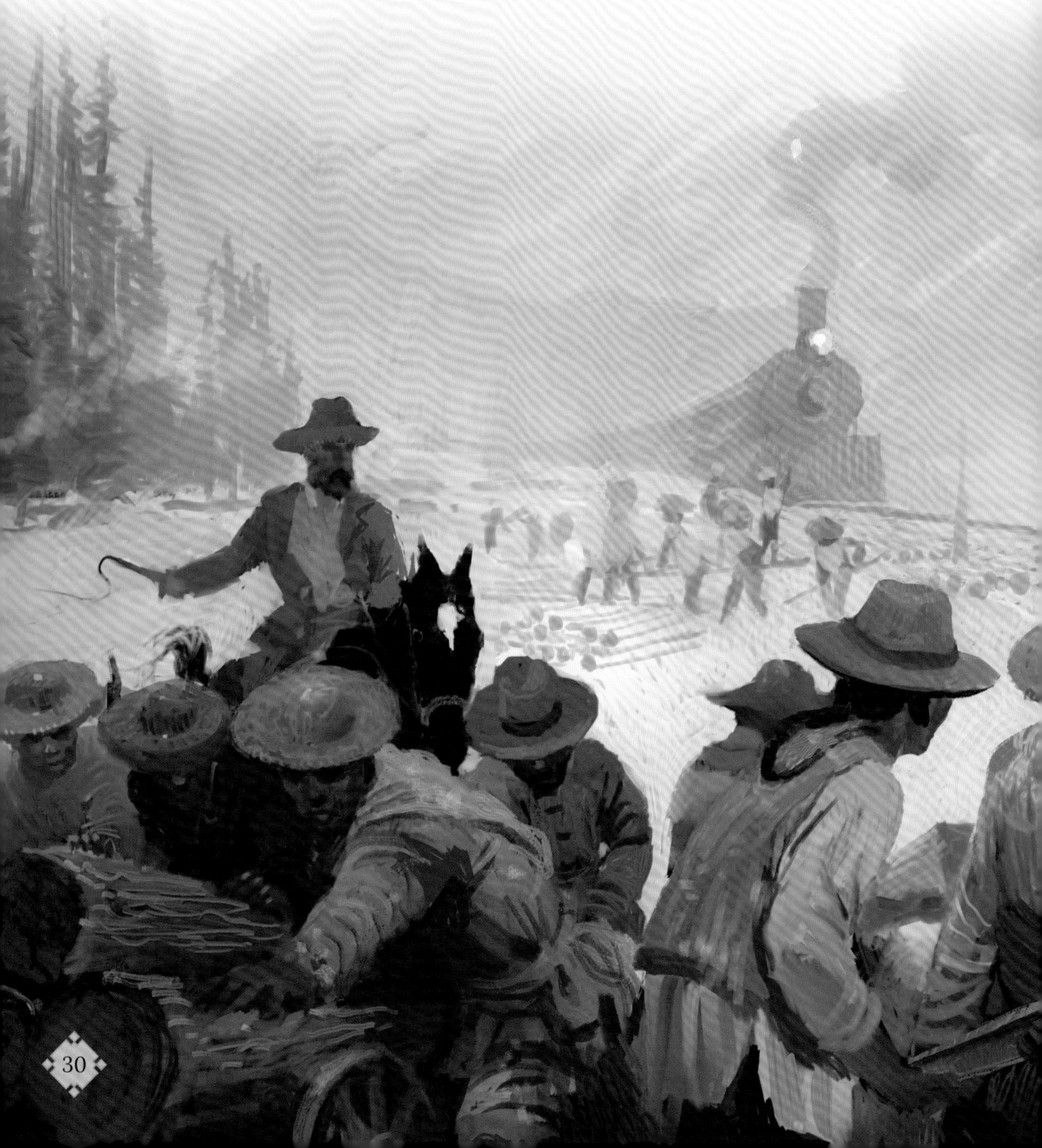

I told them that there were good people in the world. I explained that Mrs. Douglas was the wife of the late governor, and she was Métis. And I reminded them of all the other Indigenous people who had helped us survive in this new country. So many people discriminate against us, I said, but we have always had respectful relationships with the Indigenous people. They are our friends.

Over and over again, they stated, "This woman must be Guanyin, the Goddess of Mercy."

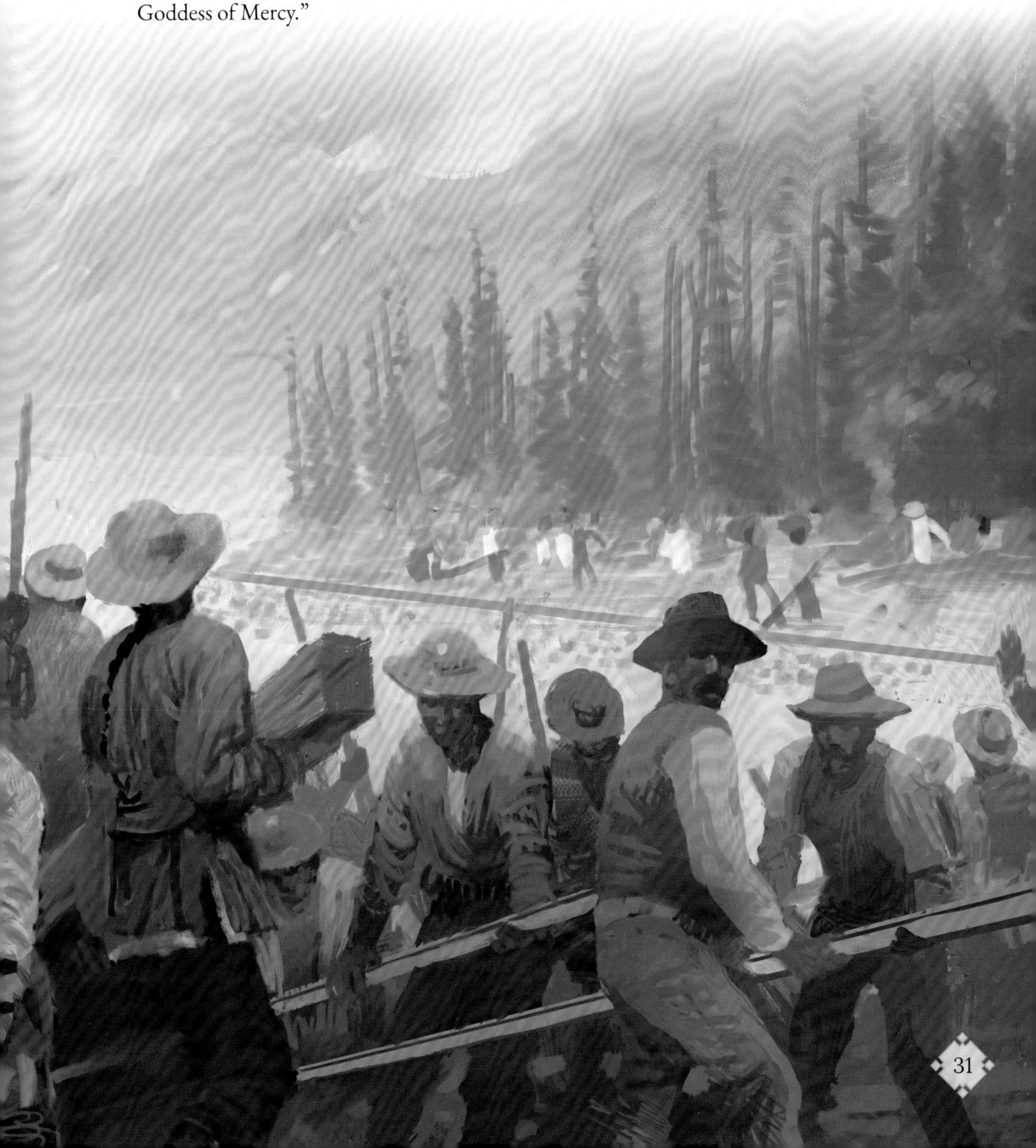

* * *

Not long after, with the railway almost complete, Chinese workers began leaving the site — some travelled north in search of gold that had been discovered there. Most of us returned to Chinatown. I went home to your grandmother and your father, and I started the business that has helped us to live this good life today.

We worked hard. With a storefront and a warehouse, we constantly hauled goods between the harbour where the ships arrived and the town. At our shop in Fan Tan Alley, we sold tea, herbs, silk, and anything else my uncle sent to us.

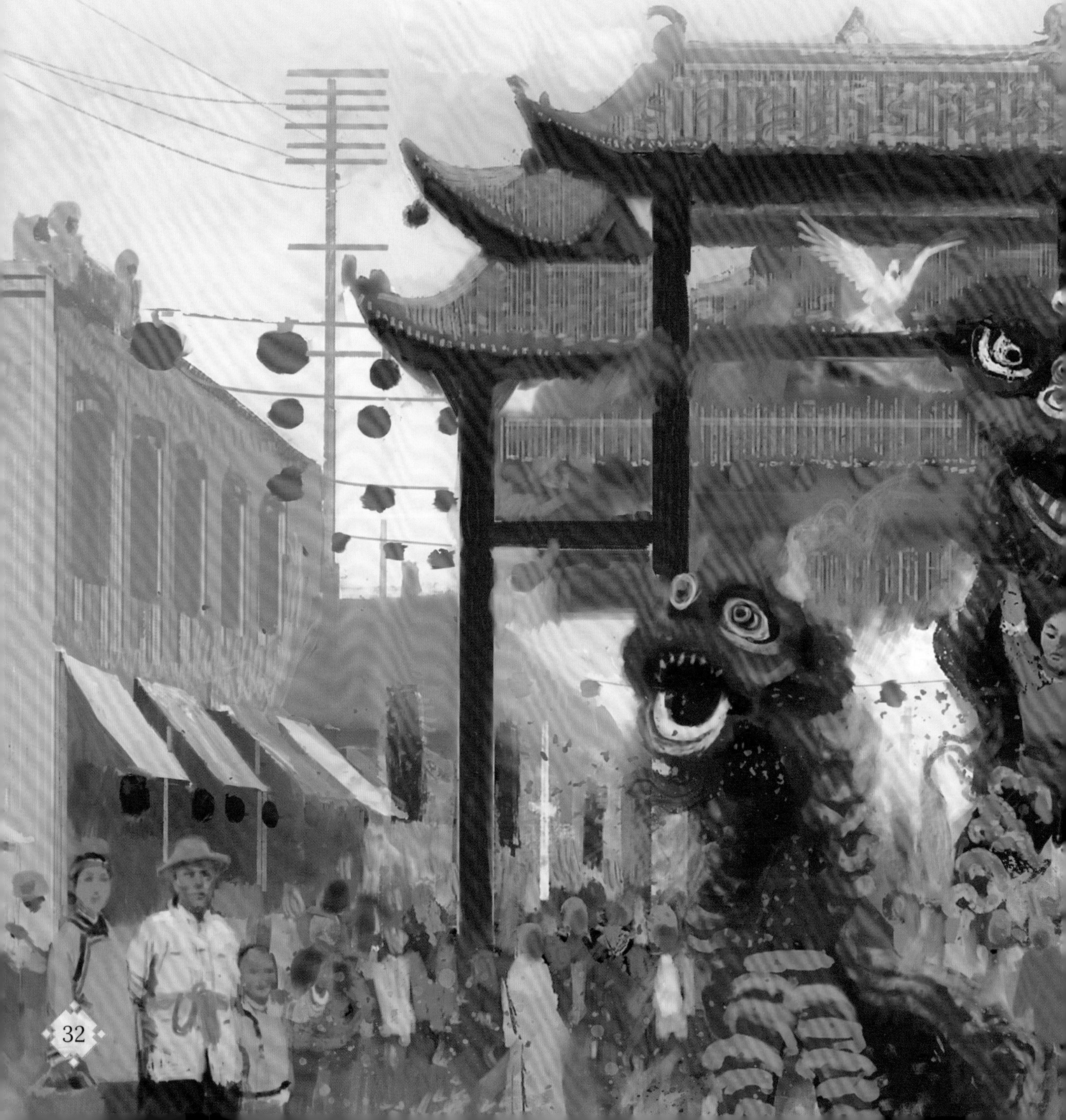

Through it all, we remembered how we had been blessed by the kindness of Mrs. Douglas. We had to do the same for other Chinese newcomers. Many came to us for food and shelter. We never refused. We knew the importance of kindness. We helped them get established. Through hard work, our people built a vibrant community of grocers and weavers, cleaners and restaurateurs, and shopkeepers of every kind.

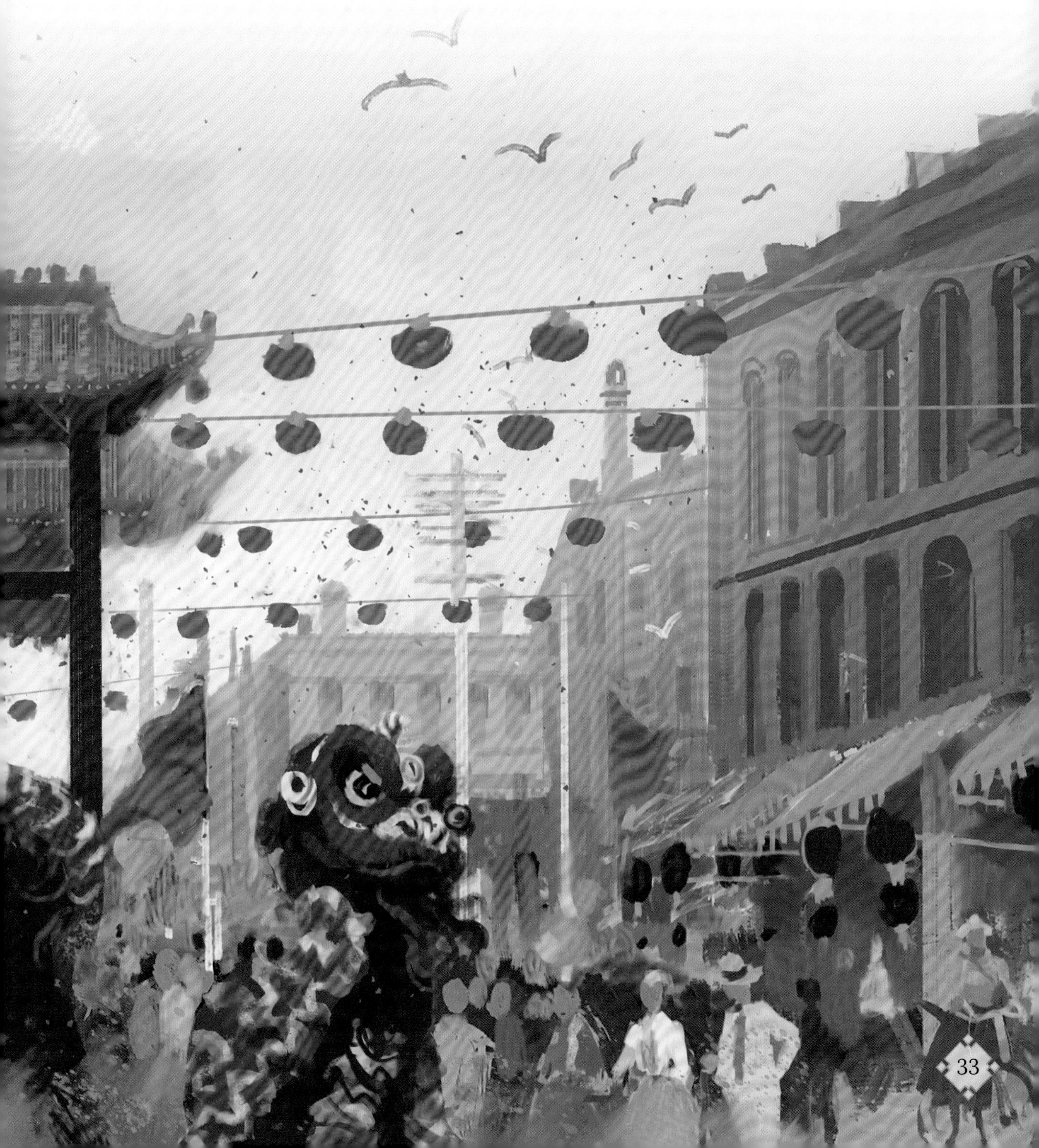

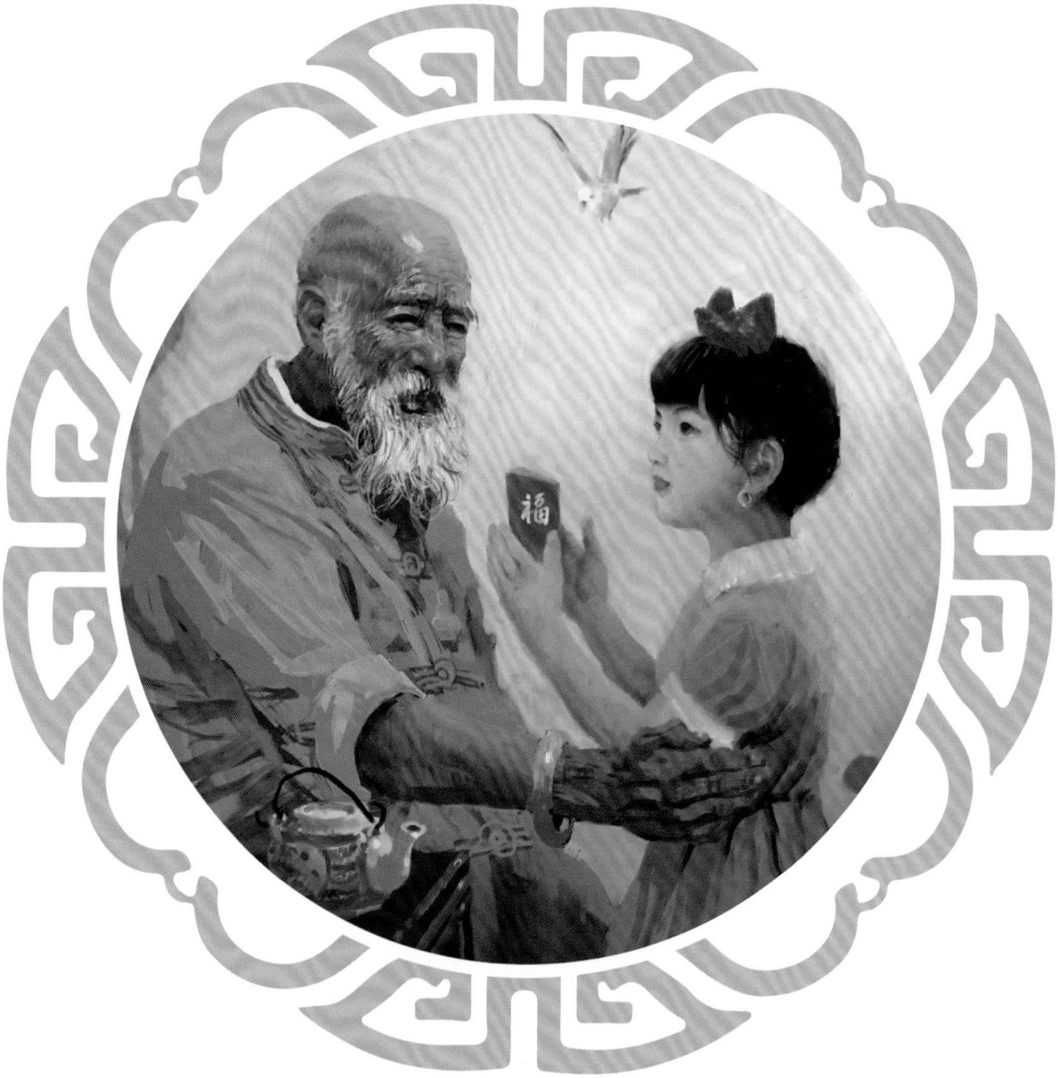
福

Granddaughter, these are your roots. This is how our family's business came to be. It is my story, and it is yours.

Granddaughter, never forget our sacrifices and our contributions to the railway that made Canada possible. Make sure that your children learn that for every mile of track laid between Vancouver and Calgary, a Chinese man lost his life. I could have been one of them, had it not been for Mrs. Douglas.

Granddaughter, always remember this woman to whom we owe our lives. Because of her, I am alive to tell you that we are proud Canadians.

~ THE END ~

HISTORICAL NOTES

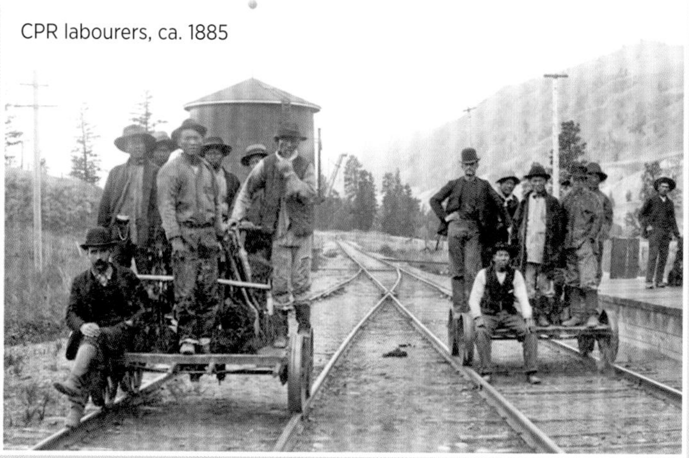
CPR labourers, ca. 1885

The Canadian Pacific Railway (CPR) was built to connect Eastern Canada to British Columbia. This railway was a promise by the Canadian government to British Columbia when it joined Confederation in 1871, becoming Canada's sixth province. Construction on the railway was started in 1881 and completed in 1885. The railway could not have been built without the labour provided by more than 15 000 temporary Chinese workers.

Why Chinese workers? Large numbers of workers were needed to work on the railway, and these workers were not available in Canada. Transporting workers from China across the Pacific Ocean to British Columbia was the easiest way to meet the need for labour. Many Chinese workers came to work on the railway in the hope of finding a better life for themselves and for their family. They soon realized that the promised land was not what it was made out to be — they were confronted with racial discrimination that made life extremely difficult.

Chinese workers were often given the most dangerous tasks, such as working with explosives. The land on which they worked was mountainous and rocky. Workers had to clear paths in order to lay tracks and ties; often this involved blasting tunnels through rock, sometimes resulting in landslides and cave-ins, causing death. Exhaustion and exposure to the elements also caused the deaths of many workers.

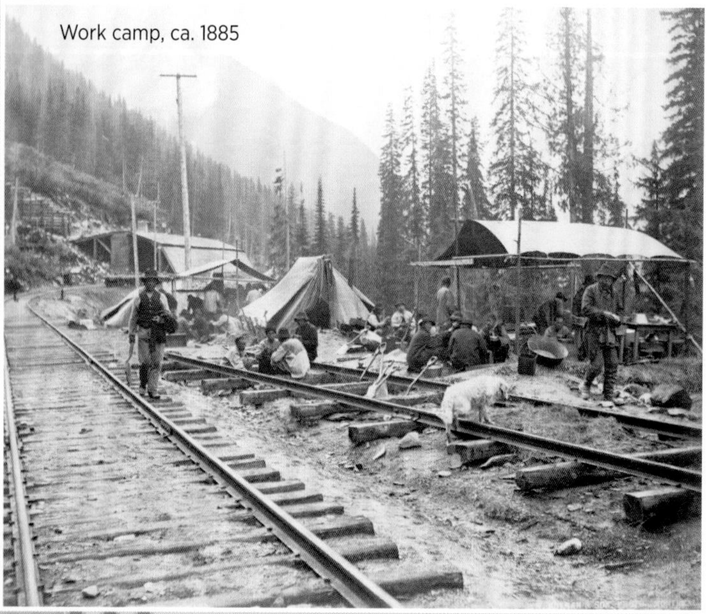
Work camp, ca. 1885

Chinese workers were paid only $1 per day and had to pay for their own food and equipment, whereas white workers were paid between $1.50 and $2.50 per day and had everything supplied to them. Chinese workers endured appalling living conditions in flimsy tents on cold mountains. Because of their low pay, they could not afford enough food, much less fresh fruit and vegetables. Many suffered from scurvy. They had no proper medical care. These factors, along with the dangerous work, caused the deaths of hundreds of Chinese workers.

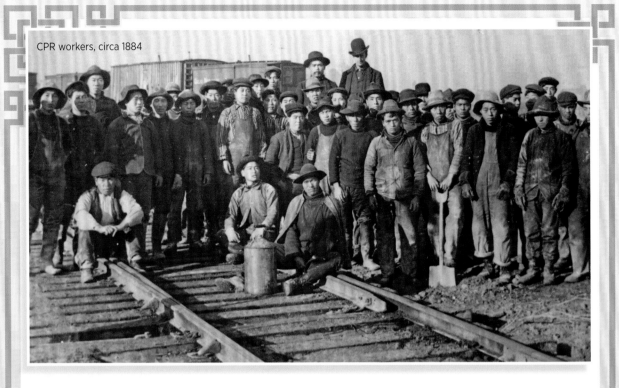
CPR workers, circa 1884

Chinese workers made up about three-quarters of the workforce on the railway, but their deaths were not included in the official accident and death tallies. In addition, the families of workers who died received no compensation and were not even notified of their deaths. It is generally believed that one Chinese worker died for every mile of track that was laid through the Rocky Mountains between Calgary and Vancouver.

The mistreatment of Chinese people did not end with the completion of the railway. When work on the railway ended, many Chinese workers stayed in British Columbia and were joined by family members and other Chinese immigrants, all hoping for a better life in Canada. In 1885, to put an end to the arrival of Chinese newcomers, the Canadian government imposed a head tax on anyone of Chinese origin entering Canada. This made it difficult for family members of the Chinese railway workers to reunite with them here. The Chinese Head Tax was removed in 1923, but in response to continuing racist sentiments, Canada instituted the Chinese Immigration Act, which made Chinese immigration to Canada extremely difficult, if not impossible. This act was not repealed until 1947.

Children on the sidewalk on Fisgard St. in Victoria's Chinatown

Despite all these racist obstructions, Chinese immigrants have succeeded — through hard work and perseverance — in becoming an important and successful part of the multicultural mosaic that today makes up Canadian society.

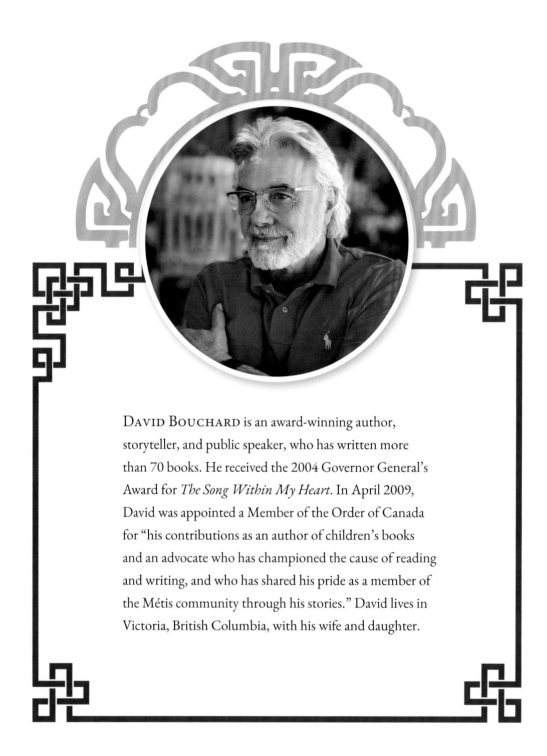

DAVID BOUCHARD is an award-winning author, storyteller, and public speaker, who has written more than 70 books. He received the 2004 Governor General's Award for *The Song Within My Heart*. In April 2009, David was appointed a Member of the Order of Canada for "his contributions as an author of children's books and an advocate who has championed the cause of reading and writing, and who has shared his pride as a member of the Métis community through his stories." David lives in Victoria, British Columbia, with his wife and daughter.

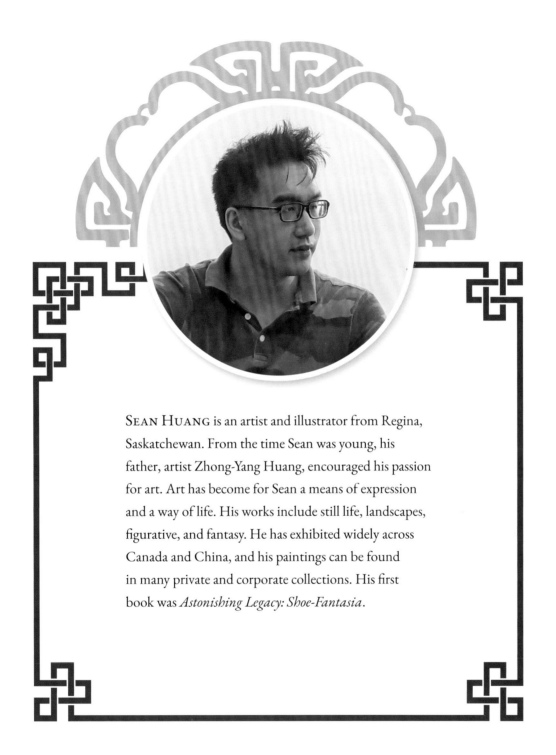

SEAN HUANG is an artist and illustrator from Regina, Saskatchewan. From the time Sean was young, his father, artist Zhong-Yang Huang, encouraged his passion for art. Art has become for Sean a means of expression and a way of life. His works include still life, landscapes, figurative, and fantasy. He has exhibited widely across Canada and China, and his paintings can be found in many private and corporate collections. His first book was *Astonishing Legacy: Shoe-Fantasia*.